The Hare and the Tortoise
with
The Sick Lion

Illustrated by Val Biro

Award Publications Limited

One sunny day, Tortoise and Hare met in the middle of a meadow.

"I can run much faster than you, Tortoise," Hare boasted proudly.

"Perhaps you can. Let's have a race and see," said Tortoise.

All the animals came to watch the race. Badger and Toad set up a starting line. Fox called out, "Ready, steady, go!"

Hare hopped off in a cloud of dust. He was soon out of sight.
Tortoise crawled slowly along – plod, plod, plod.

Hare looked behind him. He was so far ahead he could not see Tortoise. "He will never catch me!" Hare thought.
So he stopped for a rest.

He soon fell fast asleep under a shady tree.

As Hare snoozed, Tortoise slowly plodded past. "I must keep going," he said.

When Hare woke up it was too late. The animals cheered as Tortoise crossed the finish line first. "Slow and steady wins the race," he smiled.

The Sick Lion

It was a very hot day, and Lion was hungry. But he felt too hot and tired to hunt for his food.

"How can I get my dinner without running around in the sun?" he thought.

"I've got an idea!" Lion said with a grin. "My dinner can come to me instead!"

He put on his pyjamas and said in a loud voice, "Poor me! I am so ill, I must stay in bed!"

The animals heard what Lion said and they felt sorry for him.
"We should visit Lion and cheer him up," said Rabbit.

But Fox did not think Lion looked unwell. "Be careful," he warned. "It might be a trap."

Cow went to visit Lion first.

"Hello!" she called as she entered Lion's gloomy den.

The animals all thought Cow was very brave.

"I will go next," said Pig, to show he was brave too. "Hello, Lion!" he called. "Can I help you get better?"

Then Goat copied Pig. "I am sorry to hear that you are not well, Lion!" she said in her sweetest voice as she went in.

Rabbit and Duck did not feel as brave as their friends.

"Let us go to visit Lion together," said Duck. So they did just that.

The next day Fox went to see Lion. "How are you today?" he asked.

"Still poorly," croaked Lion, licking his lips, "but do come in."

"No, thank you," said Fox. He looked at the path to Lion's door and all the footprints leading in.

"I'm not a copycat," said Fox. "I can see lots of footprints going into your den, but there are none coming out. You're not going to eat me, Lion!"

And off ran clever Fox.